RICHMOND BRIDGE AND CASTLE, YORKSHIRE.

ENGLAND
100 YEARS AGO
The charm of
Victorian England illustrated

by
The Rev. Samuel Manning, LL.D.
and
The Rev. S. G. Green, D.D.

NETLEY
ABBEY.

EXCALIBUR BOOKS
NEW YORK

First published 1885
by the Religious Tract Society

This edition first published in the USA
1985 by Excalibur Books

Distributed by Bookthrift, Inc.
45 West 36th Street, New York, NY 10018

Excalibur is a trademark of Simon & Schuster Inc.
New York, New York

Bookthrift is a registered trademark of
Simon & Schuster Inc. New York, New York.
All rights reserved.

ISBN 0-671-80802-8

To complete this facsimile reprint,
the present edition also includes text and pictures
illustrative of the Principality of Wales.

Printed and bound by R. J. Acford, Chichester,
England.

WORCESTERSHIRE BEACON, MALVERN HILLS.

PREFACE.

A BRITISH nobleman— so runs the story—when travelling in Switzerland was so impressed by the gloomy grandeur of one of the mountain passes, that he exclaimed, 'Surely there is no other view like this in the world!'

'I am told, my lord,' said the guide, 'that there is but one,'—naming a view in the Scottish Highlands.

'Why,' replied the nobleman, 'that is on my own estate, and I have never seen it!'

The number of Englishmen who really know their own country is comparatively few; and no doubt there are motives quite independent of the love for natural beauty, which lead the hard-worked men of our generation to escape at intervals to as great a distance as possible from the scene of their daily occupations. The effort for this, however, often leads to yet more harassing distractions; and many return from the eager excitements of foreign travel more jaded and careworn than when they began their journey. Nor is it so easy to escape after all! The great event of the day at every Continental hotel is the arrival of *The Times;* and you are at least as likely to meet your next neighbour on a Rhine steamboat or at the Rigi Kulm, as on the Upper Thames, or at Boscastle or Tintagel.

It is true that our rivers do not flow from glaciers, and our proudest

THAMES HEAD AND HOAR STONE.

THE RIVER THAMES.

THE SEVEN SPRINGS.

THE Thames, unrivalled among English rivers in beauty as in fame, is really little known by Englishmen. Of the millions who line its banks, few have any acquaintance with its higher streams, or know them further than by occasional glances through railway-carriage windows, at Maidenhead, Reading, Pangbourne, or between Abingdon and Oxford. Multitudes, even, who love the Oxford waters, and are familiar with every turn of the banks between Folly Bridge and Nuneham, have never sought to explore the scenes of surpassing beauty where the river flows on, almost in loneliness, in its descent to London; visited by few, save by those happy travellers who, with boat and tent, pleasant companionship, and well-chosen books —Izaak Walton's *Angler* among the rest—pass leisurely from reach to reach of the silver stream. Then higher up than Oxford, who knows the Thames? Who can even tell where it arises, and through what district it flows?

There is a vague belief in many minds, fostered by some ancient manuals of geography, that the Thames is originally the Isis, so called until it receives the river *Thame*, the auspicious union being denoted by the pluralising of the latter word. The whole account is pure invention. No doubt the great river does receive the Thame or Tame, near Wallingford; but a Tame is also tributary to the Trent; and there is a Teme among the affluents of the Severn. The truth appears to be that Teme, Tame, or Thame, is an old Keltic word meaning 'smooth,' or 'broad;' and that Tamesis, of which Thames is merely a contraction, is formed by the addition to this root of the old 'Es,' water, so familiar to us in 'Ouse'[1] 'Esk,' 'Uiske,' 'Exe,' so that Tam-es means simply the 'broad water,' and is Latinised into Tamesis. The last two syllables again of this word are fancifully changed

THE FIRST BRIDGE OVER THE THAMES.

into Isis, which is thus taken as a poetic appellation of the river. In point of fact, Isis is used only by the poets, or by those who affect poetic diction. Thus Wharton, in his address to Oxford:

'Lo, your loved Isis, from the bordering vale,
With all a mother's fondness bids you hail.'

The name, then, of the Thames is singular, not plural; while yet the river is formed by many confluent streams descending from the Cotswold Hills. Which is the actual source is perhaps a question of words; and yet it is one as keenly contended, and by as many competing localities, as the birth-place of Homer was of old. Of the seven, however, only two can show a plausible case. The traditional 'Thames Head' is in Trewsbury Mead, three Miles from Cirencester. This Trewsbury Mead, the guide-books say, is 'not far from Tetbury Road Station,' on the Great Western Railway. The fact is, that there is now *no* 'Tetbury Road Station' for passengers; the traffic of antique little Tetbury having been transferred to Kemble, the junction which also serves Cirencester. There are two ways of reaching the infant Thames. One is from Kemble, where a short stroll through pleasant meadows brings the pedestrian to the river, covered—when we saw it on a bright day in early summer—with the leaves and blossoms of the water ranunculus; while a board affixed to a tree upon the bank, threatening

[1] 'The Ouse, whom men do Isis rightly name.'—SPENSER, *Faerie Queen.*

penalties to unauthorised anglers, suggested that already the Thames had won its character as a fishing stream. Not far off, a bye path from a main road near a great railway-arch is carried across the river by the *first Thames bridge*, a modest affair of three arches, on which the tourist, if disposed to a contemplation of contrasts, may stand and think of the *last* bridge that is to span the stream, the wonderful structure now rising by the Tower of London.

Should the visitor follow the course of the dwindling stream through the meadows, he will by-and-by find himself near the high embankment of the Thames and Severn Canal, in its day a work of great enterprise and utility, and still occasionally used as a link between the two famous rivers. But he will do better to return to the junction and proceed to Cirencester :

'Our town of Cicester in Gloucestershire,'

as Shakespeare has it, in the last act of *King Richard the Second*, so perpetuating a local pronunciation rapidly falling into disuse. The town itself, among its verdant rolling uplands, is worth a day's visit, even apart from its association with the Thames. Once, perhaps because of its position near the source of the great river, Cirencester was the centre of Roman civilisation and luxury in this island. To the city of Corinium, as it was then called, from the ancient British name Caer Corin, four of the chief Roman roads converged : the Fosse Way from the north-east, Akeman Street from the south-west, and Ermine Street intersecting them from the south-east and north-west, while Icknield Street passed at a little distance to the east. These roads, turned into good English turnpikes (if we may use a word which our successors will hardly understand), running in long straight lines through the undulating landscape, after the Roman fashion, are still a prominent feature in the scene. Cirencester itself has almost lost the aspect of a Roman city, save in some green mounds, revealing to an antiquary's eye the ancient earthworks, and still occasionally yielding to the delver pieces of pottery, coins, and other relics ; as well as in the very manifest lines of a considerable amphitheatre, now called the Bull Ring. The chief Roman remains from time to time discovered are preserved in the Corinium Museum, close to the railway station, a collection well catalogued and admirably kept, containing statuettes, pottery, and household implements of all kinds, vividly illustrating every feature of Roman provincial life in Britain. Two remarkably fine tesselated pavements, with hunting and other scenes, disinterred in the centre of the town about forty years ago, occupy the central floor of the museum, one of them having unfortunately been much injured in removal. The sculptor Westmacott says of them : ' Here is grandeur of form, dignity of character, and great breadth of treatment, which strongly reminds one of the finest Greek schools.'

A three or four miles' drive along the old Akeman Street takes the visitor to a point in the road where the high embankment of the canal comes into full view, crossing the meadows on the left. On the right, the church tower of Coates (the name being, no doubt, connected with *Cotswold*) is seen among the trees. Here, we are told, rises the Thames. But where? A peasant appears from a roadside cottage to explain. 'People come here,' he says, 'in the summer, when there is no water, and go away saying that there is naught to see. They should come in the winter, and see how these meadows are all flooded!' The fact is, that the traditional source of the Thames is in a deep spring, below a mound covered with trees and brush-wood, and with the stones of a ruined well. In summer weather no water comes to the surface, in rainy seasons and in winter it often breaks forth and dispreads itself over the meadows before it finds any regular channel. In fact, the first sign of the existence of any spring whatever, when we visited the spot, was in a pumping-engine on the towing-path of the embankment, some three-quarters of a mile from 'Thames Head,' which was in full activity, raising water from the deep underground store to supply the canal. The water appeared of crystal purity as it welled forth from the ugly little engine-house in continual ripples on the dull and weedy stream. This novel illustration of 'infant labour' was almost a painful one; at any rate it formed an impressive comment on the reported saying of Brindley the engineer, that 'the great use of rivers is to feed canals.' Half-a-mile farther down, when clear of the pumping-engine, the baby river issues again to light, and wanders at its own sweet will, where we met it in our walk from Kemble. The cut at the head of this chapter delineates its early course, and shows 'the Hoar Stone,' an ancient boundary, mentioned in a charter of King Æthelstan, A.D. 931.

As we have already hinted, however, there is another claimant to the honour of being the source of the Thames, in 'the Seven Springs' at Cubberley, near Cheltenham, ten miles higher up than Coates. The question is one rather of words than of hydrography; and certainly the appellation of the Thames in old charters, as well as the immemorial names of lands adjacent to Coates, as 'Thames Meadow,' 'Thames Furlong,' and the like, seem to show that this is the recognised fountain-head of the river. On the other hand, the stream that rises at Cubberley is on higher ground and further from the mouth of the river. Only, it is called 'the Churn.' It also runs southwards to Cirencester; and at Lechlade, ten miles further on, the two unite.

Whether 'the Churn' be the true Thames or not, the drive from Cheltenham to the Seven Springs is not one to be neglected by any tourist who may be so fortunate as to find himself in that town of leafy trees and fair gardens on a bright day in early summer. The longer but the finer road sweeps round the magnificent escarpment of Leckhampton Hill, one of the finest points of view in the Cotswolds. Here, beneath the crest of the

WINDSOR.

hill, the tourist is sure to have his attention called to an irregular column or pile of rocks, called from time immemorial the Devil's Chimney. It has probably been separated from the oolitic mass by the action of water washing away the softer and more friable parts of the rock. The impression can

DEVIL'S CHIMNEY, LECKHAMPTON.

scarcely be resisted that, in the broken line of the Cotswolds along this route there is a pre-historic line of cliffs, the boundary of a vast channel, with its bays and headlands, what is now the valley of the Severn having been an arm of the sea, and the Malvern Hills being heights upon the c

WOODS AND RIVER; CLIEFDEN.

For ourselves, our business is not to angle, but to observe. As we row past these grave and solemn men, absorbed in the endeavour to hook a dace or gudgeon, and recognise among them one or two of the hardest workers in London, we feel, at any rate, that the familiar sneer about 'a rod with a line at one end, and a fool at the other,' may not be altogether just.[1]

Passing a series of verdant lawns, sloping to the river's brink, we reach Mapledurham and Purley, on opposite sides of the river at one of its most exquisite bends. The former place is celebrated by Pope as the retreat of his ladye love Martha Blount, when

'She went to plain-work, and to purling brooks,
    Old-fashioned halls, dull aunts, and croaking rooks.'

The latter was the residence of Warren Hastings during his trial, and is not to be confounded with the Purley in Surrey, where Horne Tooke wrote his celebrated *Diversions*, on the origin and history of words.

The next halting-place is Caversham, sometimes magniloquently described as 'the port of Reading.' Here the Thames widens out, as shown in the view which prefaces the present chapter; the eel-traps, or 'bucks,' extending half across the river. A little lower down, the Kennet, 'for silver eels renowned,' as Pope has it, flows in from the south-west, with its memories of the high-minded and chivalrous Falkland, who fell at the battle of Newbury, on the banks of this river. Then the Loddon enters the Thames from the south, between Shiplake and Wargrave. The picturesque churches of these two villages are soon passed, and we enter the fine expanse of Henley Reach, famous in boat-racing annals. Here for many years the University matches were rowed before their removal to Putney. No sheet of water

---

[1] As we write, the following letter to the *Times* arrests our attention; it is too graphic, as well as accurate, to be lost :—

'I will not tell you where I am, except that I am staying at an hotel on the banks of the River Thames. I hesitate to name the place, charming as it is, because I am sure, when its beauties are known, it will be hopelessly vulgarised. Mine host, the pleasantest of landlords, his wife, the most agreeable of her sex, will charge, too, in proportion as the plutocracy invade us. I am surrounded by the most charming scenery. Few know, and still fewer appreciate the beauties of our own River Thames. I have been up and down the Rhine; but I confess, taking all in all, Oxford to Gravesend pleases me more. Here, in addition to what I have described, I am on the river's brink; I can row about to my heart's content for a very moderate figure; excellent fishing; newspapers to be procured, and postal arrangements of a character not to worry you, and yet sufficient to keep you *au fait* with your business arrangements. What do I want more? Prices are moderate, the village contains houses suitable to all classes, and the inhabitants are pleased to see you. I can wear flannels without being stared at, and I can see the opposite sex, in the most bewitching and fascinating of costumes, rowing about (with satisfaction, too) the so-called lords of creation. As for children, there is no end of amusement for them—dabbling in the water, feeding the swans, the fields, and the safety of a punt. We have both aristocratic and well-to-do people here—names well known in town; but I must not, nor will I, betray them. On the towing-path this morning was to be seen the smartest of our judges in a straw hat and a tourist suit, equally becoming to him as it was well cut.

'Let me advise all your readers who are hesitating where to go not to overlook the natural beauties of our River Thames. There are one or two steamers that make the journey up and down the river in three days, stopping at various places, and giving ample opportunity for passengers both to see and appreciate the scenery.

'E. C. W.'

C 2

could be better suited to the purpose, and the change is regretted by many boating-men.

We are now approaching the point at which the beauty of the river culminates. From Marlow, past Cookham, Hedsor and Cliefden, to Maidenhead, a distance of eight or ten miles, we gladly suspend the labour of the oar, and let the boat drift slowly with the stream. As we glide along, even this gentle motion is too rapid, and we linger on the way to feast our eyes upon the infinitely varied combination of chalk cliff and swelling hill and luxuriant foliage which every turn of the river brings to view :

> 'Woods, meadows, hamlets, farms,
> Spires in the vale and towers upon the hills ;
> The great chalk quarries glaring through the shade,
> The pleasant lanes and hedgerows, and those homes
> Which seemed the very dwellings of content
> And peace and sunshine.' [1]

The 'castled crags' of the Rhine and the Moselle,—the 'blue rushing of the arrowy Rhone,'—the massive grandeur of the banks of the Danube, are far more imposing and stimulating ; but the quiet, tranquil loveliness of this part of the Thames may make good its claim to take rank even with those world-famed rivers. There is something both unique and charming in the dry 'combes,' or fissures in the chalk ranges, rapidly descending and garnished with sweeping foliage of untrimmed beech trees. The branches gracefully bend down to the slope of the rising sward ; while, from the steepness of the angle, the tree-tops appear from below as a succession of pinnacles against the sky. Many a roamer through distant lands has come home to give the palm for the perfection of natural beauty to the rocks and hanging woods of Cliefden. That they are within an hour's run of London does not indeed abate their claim to admiration, but may suggest the reason why they are so comparatively little known.

Maidenhead is on the other side of the river ; Taplow opposite. The bridge between them—one of Brunel's works, will be noted for its enormous span ; its elliptical brick arches being, it is said, the widest of the kind in the world. From this point, if the beauty decreases, the historical interest becomes greater at every turn. First we pass the village and church of Bray. The scenery here is of little interest ; but it is impossible not to give a thought to 'the Vicar,' Symond Symonds, commemorated in song. Let it be noted, however, that the lyrist has used a poetic licence in his dates. The historian, Thomas Fuller, tells the story : 'The vivacious vicar, living, under King Henry VIII., Edward VI., Queen Mary, and Queen Elizabeth, was first a Papist, then a Protestant, then a Papist, then a Protestant again. He had seen some martyrs burnt (two miles off), at Windsor, and found this fire too hot for his tender temper. The vicar being taxed by one for

[1] *Down Stream to London.* By the Rev. S. J. Stone.

WIND AGAINST TIDE (TILBURY FORT).

take away the Thames too!' The words were worthy of a London citizen, and may well remind us, before we pass to other English scenes, of that which, after all, is the glory of our river. We have been dwelling chiefly on its picturesque and recreative aspects; and of these it is hardly possible to make too much, as is shown by the largely increasing number of weary brain-workers whose choicest holidays, in house-boat, fishing-punt, or tiny yacht, are found in the upper reaches of the Thames. But below the bridges of the metropolis, a new world seems to open—a busy, crowded, restless world, darkened by many a cloud of smoke, filled with strange outcries in many tongues, with unlovely ranges of building, mile after mile, until the clear water is reached at length between the marshes of Essex and the hills of Kent.

But these are only the outward aspects of the scene. Look at it in another light, and this Lower Thames inspires us with wonder and almost awe at the boundless wealth and world-wide commerce which it bears upon its ample bosom. For good or for evil, influences are going forth from these broad waters, incessantly, to affect all mankind. Ever and anon, some vessel of the yet untried 'navy of the future' looms into sight, with its grand powers of defence, its terrible possibilities of destruction. But not by these is the real power of Britain put forth. They are but a reserve. It is *another* navy that conveys the real power of our country to the nations.

Take him for all in all, the British sailor is a fine noble-hearted fellow, with faults on the surface, but a heart of oak beneath. It is not wonderful that he is the object of much benevolent and Christian attention, both ashore and afloat. Good people who want to have just a glimpse of sea-faring life, with a notion how it may be sweetened and elevated, should not be content with a cruise on the Thames, or even with a steamboat voyage. Let them brace up their energies some summer-time to go 'nor'rard of the Dogger,' and learn what the North Sea is like! For those who can stand it, here is the pearl and crown of all holidays, with bracing influence on the energies, and life-long material for thought!

But, returning to our favourite river. Of the outward-bound ships, dropping downward with the tide, there are those which convey the Missionary to his scene of hallowed toil :—

'Fly, happy, happy sails, and bear the Press,
Fly happy with the mission of the Cross.'

A friend of ours in long passed days, used to tell us of the first time he listened to Robert Hall, and of the first words which he caught from the great preacher's lips. The place of worship was crowded, and for a time the low utterances of Mr. Hall's marvellous voice were completely lost. The assembly was standing in prayer, as the custom then was. By degrees a hush crept over the throng—a silence that might be felt—then through the stillness stole the preacher's voice, in sweet and solemn continuance of his hitherto unheard supplication : *And may the breath of prayer fill the sails of every missionary ship, and waft it all over the world !*

These memories and thoughts, and 'the vision that shall be,' have led us far. The stream whose course we have traced from the tiny rivulet in Trewsbury Mead has become to our thoughts the channel of communications which, for good or evil, are affecting every nation under heaven. May He who has endowed us with such wealth and power lead us to hold them both under a deep sense of responsibility to Him who gave them !'—'Then shall our peace flow like a river, and our righteousness as the waves of the sea.'

BRIDGE OVER THE CHERWELL, AT CROPREDY.

SOUTH-EASTERN RAMBLES.

SURREY, KENT, AND SUSSEX.

caution on many points that need not be indicated here. But, well managed, it must be a moral and educational influence fraught with blessing.

We are now fairly in the Surrey Hills, and may put what some will think the very crown to these south-eastern excursions by a walk from Dorking to Farnham. Ascending by one of many lanes, shadowed (at the time of our visit) by hedges bright with hawthorn berries, and tall trees just touched with the russet and gold of early autumn, we are soon upon an upland stretch of heath and forest, still remaining in all the wildness of nature. Sometimes the path leads us between venerable trees—oak and beech, and yew, whose branches form an impenetrable roof overhead, then

COBDEN'S BIRTHPLACE, AT MIDHURST.

traverses a sweep of bare hill, bright with gorse and heather, then plunges into some fairy dell, carpeted with softest moss. Many of the 'stately homes of England' upon the lower slopes, with their embowering trees, add a charm to the scene by their reminiscences as well as by their beauty. To the left is Wotton; made famous by the name and genius of John Evelyn, author of *Sylva* and the *Diary*—the scholar, gentleman, and Christian—pure-minded in an age of corruption, and the admiration of dissolute courtiers, who could respect what they would not imitate. It is to him that Cowley says:

'Happy art thou, whom God does bless
With the full choice of thine own happiness;
And happier yet, because thou'rt blest
With wisdom how to choose the best.'

E

SHERE CHURCH.

That the choice was made, for life and death, appears by the inscription which Evelyn directed to be placed on his tombstone at Wotton. 'That living in an age of extraordinary events and revolution, he had learned from thence this truth, which he desired might be thus communicated to posterity: that all is vanity which is not honest, and that there is no solid wisdom but real piety.'

Beyond Wotton is the charming village of Shere, with its picturesque little church and crystal stream. Two or three miles farther, Albury is reached, with its lovely gardens designed by Evelyn. The curious traveller may here inspect the sumptuous church erected by the late Mr. Drummond, the owner of Albury, for the followers of Edward Irving. The worth of

Mr. Drummond's character, with the shrewd sense and caustic wit by which he was wont to enliven the debates of the House of Commons, laid a deeper hold upon his contemporaries than his theological peculiarities : and the special views of which this temple is the costly memorial have proved of insufficient power to sway the minds and hearts of men. Still ascending, we reach again the summit of steep downs, and, advancing by noble yew trees, gain at Newlands'

AT HASLEMERE.

Corner another magnificent view. The hill of the 'Holy Martyrs'' Chapel, now corrupted to 'Saint Martha's,' may next be climbed, and a short rest at the fine old town of Guildford will be welcome. The castle, the churches with their monuments, and Archbishop Abbot's Hospital, are all worthy of a visit ; and a run by rail to Haslemere, near which beautiful village Lord

Tennyson has fixed his abode, may well occupy a leisure day, with, if possible, a climb to Blackdown, a mile or two beyond the poet's residence, with its fresh breezes and splendid prospects. But for the pedestrian a much finer approach to Haslemere will be over the upland commons from Farnham. Reserving, therefore, this excursion for the present, let us press on from Guildford to Farnham by a ten miles' walk over the 'Hog's Back.'

Climbing from the Guildford station through pleasant lanes, the traveller emerges upon a narrow chalk-ridge, half-a-mile wide, and nearly level, which etymologists tell us was called by the Anglo-Saxons *Hoga*, a hill, whence the ridge received its name. Possibly, however, a simpler derivation, as the more obvious, is also the more correct. The long upland unbroken line might not inaptly have been compared with one of those long, lean, narrow-backed swine with which early English illuminations make us familiar; and the homeliness of the name would quite accord with the habit of early topographers. The walk is interesting, but, after the varied beauties of the way from Dorking to Guildford, may appear at first slightly monotonous. On either side the fair, fertile champaign of Surrey stretches to the horizon, broken here and there by low wood-crowned hills; and at one point especially, between Puttenham on the left, and Wanborough on the right, the combinations of view are very striking. Puttenham church-tower, and the manor-house, formerly the Priory, peep out from amongst the foliage of some grand old trees. A few cottages and farmhouses lie scattered about picturesquely, forming the very ideal of an old English village; while pine-covered Crooksbury Hill, with the 'Devil's Jumps' and Hindhead in the farther distance, make a striking background to the view. 'Wan' is evidently 'Woden,' and here there was no doubt a shrine of the ancient Saxon deity. We must not omit in passing to drink of the Wanborough spring, among the freshest and purest in England; never known, it is said, to freeze.

Pursuing our journey, we presently look down upon Moor Park, and Waverley, which we may either visit now, descending by the little village of Seale, or reserve for an excursion from Farnham. Waverley contains the picturesque remains of an old Cistercian Abbey, built as the Cistercians always did build, in a charming valley, embosomed in hills, irrigated by a clear running stream, abounding in fish, and with current enough to turn the mill of the monastery. The annals of this great establishment, extending over two hundred and thirty years, were published towards the close of the seventeenth century; and Sir Walter Scott took from them the name now so familiar wherever the English language is spoken.

Divided from Waverley by a winding lane, whose high banks and profuse undergrowth remind us of Devonshire, lies Moor Park. Hither Sir William Temple retired from the toils of state, to occupy his leisure by gardening, planting, and in writing memoirs. A trim garden, with stiff-clipped hedges, and watered by a straight canal which runs through it, is doubtless a remini- scence of Temple's residence as our ambassador at the Hague. 'But,' says Lord Macaulay, 'there were other inmates of Moor Park to whom a higher interest belongs. An eccentric, uncouth, disagreeable young Irishman, who had narrowly escaped plucking at Dublin, attended Sir William as an amanuensis for board and twenty pounds a year; dined at the second table,

A HOP-GARDEN.

wrote bad verses in praise of his employer, and made love to a very pretty dark-eyed young girl, who waited on Lady Giffard. Little did Temple imagine that the coarse exterior of his dependant concealed a genius equally suited to politics and to letters, a genius destined to shake great kingdoms, to stir the laughter and the rage of millions, and to leave to posterity memorials which can only perish with the English language. Little did he think that the flirtation in his servants' hall, which he, perhaps, scarcely deigned to make the subject of a jest, was the beginning of a long, un prosperous love, which was to be as widely famed as the passion of Petrarch or Abélard. Sir William's secretary was Jonathan Swift. Lady Giffard's waiting-maid was poor Stella.'

Just outside the lodge gate, at the end of the park farthest from the mansion, is a small house covered with roses and evergreens. It is known to the peasantry as 'Dame Swift's Cottage.' Our rustic guide pointed it out by this name, but who Dame Swift was he did not know. He had never heard of Stella and her sad history. An object of far greater interest to him was a large fox-earth, a couple of hundred yards away, in which some years ago 'a miser' had lived and died. A whole crop of legends have already sprung up about the mysterious inmate of the cave. He was a nobleman, so said our informant, who had been crossed in love; he had made a vow that no human being should see his face, and accordingly never came out till after nightfall, even then being closely wrapped up in his cloak. After his death a party of ladies and gentlemen came down from London in a post-chaise and four; and, having buried the body, carried away 'a cartload of golden guineas and fine dresses, which he had hid in the cave.'

The picturesqueness of the approach to Farnham, whether over the last ridge of the Hog's Back, or through the lanes from Seale, Moor Park, and Waverley, is much enhanced by the hop-gardens, which occupy about a thousand acres in the neighbourhood. For excellence the Farnham hops are considered to bear the palm, although the chief field of this peculiar branch of cultivation is in Kent. No south-eastern rambles, especially in the early autumn, would be complete without a visit to the gardens where the hop-picking is in full operation. It is the great holiday for thousands of the humbler class of Londoners, as well as the chosen resort of thousands of the 'finest pisantry' from the Emerald Isle. Costermongers, watermen, sempstresses, factory girls, labourers of all descriptions, young and old, bear a hand at the work. The air is invigorating, the task to the industrious is easy, and the pay is not bad. The hop-pickers, who are in such numbers that they cannot obtain even humble lodgings in the villages, sleep in barns, sheds, stables, and booths, or even under the hedges in the lanes. A rough kind of order is maintained among themselves; although outbreaks of violence and de- bauchery sometimes happen. On the whole, the work is not unhealthy, and the opportunity of engaging in it is as real a boon to the hop-pickers as the journey to Scarborough or Biarritz to those of another class. Besides which, the great gathering of people gives opportunities of which Christian activity avails itself; and the evening visit to the encampment, the homely address, the quiet talk, and the well-chosen tract, have been instrumental of lasting good to those whom religious agencies elsewhere have failed to reach.

Farnham has special associations with both the Church and the Army; and the impartial visitor will no doubt take an opportunity of seeing the stately moated castle, the abode of the Bishops of Winchester, and of visiting

CROUCH OAK, ADDLESTONE.

the neighbouring camp of Aldershot. The politician will recall the name of William Cobbett, who was born in this neighbourhood, and, in his own direct and homely style, often dwells on his boyish recollections of its charms. Some will not forget another name associated with this little Surrey town.

One among the sweetest singers of our modern Israel, Augustus Toplady, was born at Farnham. He died at the age of thirty-eight, but he lived long enough to write 'Rock of Ages, cleft for me;' and none need covet a nobler earthly immortality.

From Farnham, as we have said, the pedestrian may pursue his way over breezy uplands by Hindhead and the 'Devil's Punchbowl' to Haslemere —a grand and inspiring nine miles' walk: or he may return, as we were fain to do, by rail to London, only turning aside at Weybridge to Addlestone to see the Crouch Oak—one of the famous trees of England. *Crouch* perhaps means *cross*, from some mark upon the tree, once showing it to be on the boundary of Windsor Forest. But however this may be, the tree is a grand relic of the past. John Wycliffe, it is said, once preached under its spreading branches; and a better-attested tradition represents 'the good Queen Bess' as having once dined beneath its shadow.

WINDMILL NEAR ARUNDEL.

OUR FORESTS AND WOODLANDS.

IN THE NEW FOREST.

'The groves were God's first temples. Ere man learned
To hew the shaft, and lay the architrave,
And spread the roof above them,—ere he framed
The lofty vault, to gather and roll back
The sound of anthems; in the darkling wood,
Amid the cool and silence, he knelt down,
And offered to the Mightiest solemn thanks
And supplication.'

WILLIAM CULLEN BRYANT.

THE NEW FOREST.—A GROUP OF FOREST PONIES.

OUR FORESTS AND WOODLANDS

WHEN Britain was first brought by Roman ambition within the know-
ledge of Southern Europe, the interior of our island was one vast
forest. Cæsar and Strabo agree in describing its towns as being nothing more
than spaces cleared of trees—'royds,' or 'thwaites,' in North of England
phrase—where a few huts were placed and defended by ditch or rampart.
Somersetshire and the adjacent counties were covered by the Coit Mawr, or
Great Wood. Asser tells us that Berkshire was so called from the Wood
of Berroc, where the box-tree grew most abundantly. Buckinghamshire was
so called from the great forests of beech (*boc*), of which the remnants still
survive. The Cotswold Hills, and the Wolds of Yorkshire, are shown by
their names to have been once far-spreading woodlands; and the same may
be said of the Weald of Sussex, the subject, in part, of the preceding chapter.
'In the district of the Weald,' writes the Rev. Isaac Taylor, 'almost every
local name, for miles and miles, terminates in *hurst, ley, den,* or *field*. The
hursts were the dense portions of the forests; the *leys* are the open forest-
glades where the cattle love to lie; the *dens* are the deep-wooded valleys, and
the *fields* were little patches of "felled" or cleared land in the midst of the
surrounding forest. From Petersfield and Midhurst, by Billinghurst, Cuckfield,
Wadhurst, and Lamberhurst as far as Hawkshurst and Tenterden, these
names stretch in an uninterrupted string.' And, again, 'A line of names
ending in *den* testifies to the existence of the forest tract in Hertfordshire,
Bedfordshire, and Huntingdon, which formed the western boundary of the
East Saxon and East Anglian Kingdom. Henley in Arden and Hampton
in Arden are vestiges of the great Warwickshire forest of Arden, which

stretched from the Forest of Dean to Sherwood Forest.'[1] Hampshire was already a forest in the time of William the Conqueror; all he did was to sweep away the towns and villages which had sprung up within its precincts. Epping and Hainault are but fragments of the ancient forest of Essex, which extended as far as Colchester. Lancashire, Cheshire, Yorkshire and the other northern counties, were the haunts of the wolf, the wild boar, and the red deer, which roamed at will over moorland and forest, and have given their names here and there to a bold upland or sequestered nook.

Even down to the time of Queen Elizabeth immense tracts of primeval forest remained unreclaimed. Sir Henry Spelman[2] gives the following list of those which were still in existence.

FOREST.	COUNTY.	FOREST.	COUNTY.
Applegarth	York.	Knuckles	Radnor.
Arundel	Sussex.	Leicester	Leicester.
Ashdown	. . .	St. Leonards	Sussex.
Bere	Hants.	Lounsdael	. . .
Birnwood	Bucks.	Lowes	Northumberland.
Blackmore	Wilts.	Lune	York.
Blethnay	Radnor.	Lyfield	Rutland.
Bowland (*Pendle*)	Lancashire.	Mactry	Salop.
Bredon	Wilts.	Mallustary	Westmoreland.
Bucholt	Hants.	Narberth	Pembroke.
Cantrelly	. . .	New Forest	Hants.
Cardith	Caermarthen.	New Forest	York.
Char	Hants.	Peak	Derby.
Charnwood	Leicester.	Pemshaur	Wilts.
Chut	Wilts.	Pickering	York.
Coidrath	Pembroke.	Radnor	Radnor.
Copland	Cumberland.	Rockingham	Northampton.
Dallington	Sussex.	Ruscob	Cardigan.
Dartmore	Devon.	Salcey	Northampton.
Dean	Gloucester.	Savernack	Wilts.
Delamere	Chester.	Sapler	. . .
Derefield	Salop.	Selwood	Somerset and Wilts.
Downe	Sussex.	Sherwood	Nottingham.
Exmere	Devon.	Waltham	Essex.
Feckenham	. . .	Waybridge	Huntingdon.
The Forest	Cardigan.	West Forest	Hants.
Fromulwood	Somerset.	West Ward	Cumberland.
Gaiternack	Wilts.	Wheigthart	. . .
Gautries	York.	Whichwood	Oxford.
Gillingham	Dorset.	Whinfield	Westmoreland.
Harwood	Salop.	Whitney	. . .
Hatfield	Essex.	Whittlewood	Northampton.
Haye	. . .	Windsor	Berks.
Holt	Dorset.	Wolmerwood	York.
Huestoun	. . .	Worth	Sussex.
Inglewood	Cumberland.	Wutmer	Hants.
Kingswood	Gloucester.	Wyersdale	Lancashire.
Knaresboro'	York.		

[1] *Words and Places*, pp. 381-3. [2] Quoted in *English Forests and Forest Trees.*

This list is evidently far from complete. It may, however, serve to show the extent of unreclaimed land in England so recently as the sixteenth century. And here it should be noted that though, as a matter of fact, forest lands are generally woodlands also, this is not essential to the meaning of the word. A 'forest,' says Mr. Hensleigh Wedgwood,[1] 'is probably a wilderness, or uncultivated tract of country; but, as such were commonly overgrown with trees, the word took the meaning of a large wood. We have many forests in England without a stick of timber upon them.' It is especially so in Scotland, as many a traveller who has driven all the long day by the treeless 'Forest of Breadalbane' will well remember.

The question has been recently much discussed whether our forests ought to be retained in their present extent. Economists have shown by calculation that forests do not pay. It is said that they encourage idleness and poaching, and thus lead to crime. Estimates have been made of the amount of corn which might be raised if the soil were brought under the plough. Yet few persons who have wandered through the glades of our glorious woodlands would be willing to part with them. Admit that the cost of maintenance is in excess of their return to the national exchequer, yet England is rich enough to bear the loss; and it is a poor economy which reduces everything to a pecuniary estimate. 'Man shall not live by bread alone.' In God's world beauty has its place as well as utility. 'Consider the lilies.'

> 'God might have made enough—enough
>   For every want of ours,
> For temperance, medicine, and use,
>   And yet have made no flowers.'

'He hath made everything beautiful in its time;' and intends that we should rejoice in His works as well as feed upon His bounty and learn from His wisdom. While by no means insensible to the charm of a richly cultivated district, where 'the pastures are clothed with flocks, the valleys also are covered over with corn,' yet let us trust that the day is far distant when our few remaining forests shall have disappeared before modern improvements and scientific husbandry.

To the lover of nature, forest scenery is beautiful at all seasons. How pleasant is it, in the hot summer noon, to lie beneath the 'leafy screen,' through which the sunlight flickers like golden rain; to watch the multitudinous life around us—the squirrel flashing from bough to bough, the rabbit darting past with quick, jerky movements, the birds flitting hither and thither in busy idleness, the columns of insects in ceaseless, aimless, gliding motion—and to listen to the mysterious undertone of sound which pervades rather than disturbs the silence! Beautiful, too, are the woods when autumn has touched their greenery with its own variety of hue. From the old

[1] *Dictionary of English Etymology.*

On other parts of England's forest scenery, only less noteworthy than the above, we must not now linger.

The tourist who has a day or two at disposal may well combine with his New Forest excursions a visit to SALISBURY PLAIN, and especially to Stonehenge, that unique and mysterious British sanctuary. The Plain itself is not what many travellers expect to find. In literature it appears far more desolate and sterile than it will actually be found. Nor is it a level expanse such as its name suggests. Once it was a bare wind-swept un-dulating plateau, with innumerable tumuli, and barrows often marked by clumps of trees. The barrows and tumuli remain, silent memorials of nameless warriors and forgotten armies. But the barrenness has given way to cultivation; and, though many parts of the widespread tract are bleak enough in the wild winds of spring and autumn, there is not much to distinguish the plain from other rural scenes where an open country is dotted over with well-kept farms, wide pasture lands, and villages sheltered in leafy hollows. A pleasant breezy drive leads from Salisbury, past the grassy mound of Old Sarum, by Amesbury and 'Vespasian's Camp,' towards the quiet hill-brow where the grey stones of the Druid monument stand out against the horizon. To the unpractised eye they at first appear small— almost insignificant—in contrast with the great sweep of the surrounding plain; but on approaching them we apprehend their vastness. After a time it becomes easy to reconstruct in thought the circles of the great temple; somewhat helped, perhaps, by the pictures of Stonehenge as restored, which the visitor will find offered for sale on the spot. But of the mystery there is no solution, excepting that some connection with sun-worship is proved by one significant circumstance. From the central slab, or 'altar,' along one of the avenues, a small stone is seen at some distance outside the circle, and this proves to be exactly in a line between the altar and the point of sunrise on the longest day. Such coincidence can hardly be accidental; but what it precisely signifies no records exist to show.

Passing now westwards, we reach the FOREST OF DEAN, less extensive than the New Forest, but hardly less beautiful,—

'The queen of forests all that west of Severn lie.'—*Drayton.*

It occupies the high ground between the valleys of the Severn and the Wye. What Lyndhurst is to the one, the Speech House is to the other. The Foresters' Courts have been held here for centuries, in a large hall panelled with dark oak and hung round with deer's antlers. Here the 'verderers,' foresters, 'gavellers,' miners, and Crown agents meet to discuss in open court their various claims in a sort of local parliament. Originally the King's Lodge, it is now a comfortable inn, affording good accommodation for the lovers of sylvan scenery. The deer with which the forest once abounded diminished in numbers up to 1850, when they were removed. But, as in the New

Forest, droves of ponies and herds of swine roam at large among the trees, giving animation and interest to the landscape. A different feeling is aroused by the sight of furnaces and coal-pits in different directions, indicative of the mineral treasures hidden beneath the fair surface of this forest. Ironworks have in fact existed here from very early times; the forest trees having, as in the Weald of Sussex, afforded an abundant supply of fuel, though (thanks to the coal-beds beneath) without the same result in denuding the district of its leafy glories.

SAVERNAKE FOREST, in Wiltshire, the property of the Marquis of Ailesbury, is the only English forest belonging to a subject, and is especially remarkable for its avenues of trees. One, of magnificent beeches, is nearly four miles in length, and is intersected at one point of its course by three separate 'walks,' or forest vistas, placed at such angles as, with the avenue itself, to command eight points of the compass. The effect is unique and beautiful, the artificial character of the arrangement being amply compensated by the exceeding luxuriance of the thick-set trees, and the soft loveliness of the verdant flowery glades which they enclose. The smooth bright foliage of the beech is interspersed with the darker shade of the fir, while towering elms and majestic wide-spreading oaks diversify the line of view in endless, beautiful variety. At one point, a clump of trees will be reached—the veterans of the forest, with moss-clad trunks and gnarled half-leafless branches; the chief being known as the King Oak, but sometimes called the Duke's, from the Lord Protector Somerset, with whom this tree was a favourite. The railway from Hungerford to Marlborough skirts this forest, the southern portion of which is known as Tottenham Park. An obelisk, erected on one of its highest points, in 1781, to commemorate the recovery of George III., forms an easily-recognisable landmark, and may also guide the wanderer in the forest glades, who might else be bewildered by the very uniformity of the long lines of foliage. On the whole, if this Forest of Savernake has not the vast extent or the wild natural beauty of some other forests, it has all the charm that the richest luxuriance can give; while some of its noblest trees will be found away from the great avenues, on the gentle slopes or in the mossy dells which diversify the surface of this most beautiful domain. Nor will the visitor in spring-time fail to be delighted by the great banks of rhododendron and azalea, which at many parts add colour and splendour to the scene.

Among our smaller woodlands, the BURNHAM BEECHES claim special notice. They are reached by a charming drive of five or six miles from Maidenhead. The road leads at first through one of the most highly-cultivated and fertile districts in England, and then enters Dropmore Park, with its stately avenues of cedar and pine, and some of the finest araucarias in Europe. The Beeches occupy a knoll which rises from the plain, over which it commands splendid views, Windsor Castle and the valley of the Thames being conspicuous

BURNHAM.

objects in the landscape. The trees are many of them of immense girth; but having been pollarded—tradition says by Cromwell's troopers—they do not attain a great height. They are thus wanting in the feathery grace and sweep which form the characteristic beauty of the beech; but, in exchange for this, the gnarled, twisted branches are in the very highest degree picturesque, and to the wearied Londoner few ways of spending a summer's day can be more enjoyable than a ramble over the Burnham Knoll, with its turfy slopes and shaded dells, or, better still, a picnic with some chosen friends in the shadow of one or other of these stupendous trees.

Space will not allow us to do more than refer to the forests of EPPING and HAINAULT, so invaluable to wearied Londoners; or of SHERWOOD, with its memories of Robin Hood and his 'merry men;' or of CHARNWOOD, with its wooded heights and picturesque ruins; or of NEEDWOOD, between the Dove and the Trent; or of WHITTLEBURY and DELAMERE, with many others. The names recall the memories of happy days spent beneath their leafy screen, or in wandering over breezy heights, with grateful thoughts of—

'That unwearied love
Which planned and built, and still upholds this world,
So clothed with beauty for rebellious man.'

NEEDWOOD FOREST

SHAKSPERE'S COUNTRY.

authentic relic, suggests many a thought of the great brain which it once enclosed; and, while other items in the antique show pass as phantasmagoria before the bewildered attention, there are some portraits on the walls to have seen which is a lasting pleasure of memory. It is a happy thing that these were spared by the fire of 1871; justly counted as a national calamity rather than a family misfortune. The traces of the conflagration are now almost wholly removed, although some priceless treasures have been irrecoverably lost. At the lodge, by the castle gate, there is a museum of curiosities, which will interest the believers in the great 'Guy,' and will amuse others. For there is the giant's 'porridge pot' of bell-metal, vast in circumference and resonant in ring; with his staff, his horse's armour, and, to crown all,

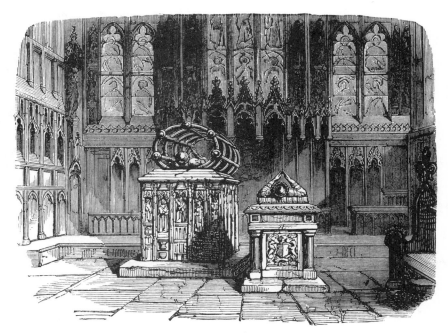

BEAUCHAMP CHAPEL, ST. MARY'S CHURCH, WARWICK.

some ribs of the 'dun cow' herself! What if, in sober truth, some last lingerer of a species now extinct roamed over the great forest of Arden, the terror of the country, until Sir Guy wrought deliverance?

Warwick itself need not detain us long; the church, however, demands a visit; and the Beauchamp Chapel, with its monuments, is one of the finest in England. But the pedestrian will probably elect to spend the night at Leamington, close by, before continuing his pilgrimage. A visit to the beautiful Jephson Gardens, with their wealth of evergreen oaks, soft turfy lawn, and broad fair water, will afford him a pleasant evening; and the next morning will see him *en route* for Stratford-on-Avon. Again let him take the road, drinking in the influence of the pleasant Warwickshire scene: quiet

G

rural loveliness, varying with every mile, and glimpses of the silver Avon at
intervals, enhancing the charm.   A slight détour will lead to Hampton Lucy,
and Charlecote House and Park, memorable for the exploits of Shakspere's

LEICESTER'S HOSPITAL, WARWICK.

youth, and for the worshipful dignity of Sir Thomas Lucy, the presumed
original of Mr. Justice Shallow.   The park having been skirted, or crossed,
the tourist proceeds three or four miles farther by a good road, and enters

STRATFORD-ON-AVON CHURCH.

Stratford-on-Avon by a stone bridge of great length, crossing the Avon and adjacent low-lying meadows. The bridge, which dates from the reign of Henry VII., has been widened on an ingenious plan, by a footpath supported on a kind of iron balcony. It is easy, however, to imagine its exact appearance when Shakspere paced its narrow roadway, or hung over its parapet to watch the skimming swallow or the darting trout and minnow.

This Warwickshire town has been so often and so exhaustively described that we may well forbear from any minute detail. Every visitor knows, with tolerable accuracy, what he has to expect. He finds, as he had anticipated, a quiet country town, very much like other towns; neither obtrusively modern, nor quaintly antique—in one word, commonplace, save for the all-pervading presence and memory of Shakspere. The house in Henley Street, where he is said to have been born, will be first visited, of course; then the tourist will walk along the High Street, noting the Shakspere memorials in the shop-windows, looking up as he passes to the fine statue of the poet, placed by Garrick in front of the Town Hall. At the site of New Place, now an open, well-kept garden, with here and there some of the shattered foundations of the poet's house, protected by wire-work, on the greensward, the visitor will add his tribute of wonder, if not of contempt, to the twin memories of Sir Hugh Clopton, who pulled down Shakspere's house in one generation, and of the Rev. Francis

STATUE OF SHAKSPERE IN FRONT OF STRATFORD
TOWN HALL.

Gastrell, who cut down Shakspere's mulberry-tree in another. Just opposite are the guild chapel, the guildhall, with the grammar school where the poet, no doubt, received his education; and, after some further walking, the extremity of the town will be reached, where a little gate opens to a charming avenue of overarching lime-trees, leading to the church. Before he enters, let him pass round to the other side, where the churchyard gently slopes to the Avon, and drink in the tranquillity and beauty of the rustic scene. Then, after gaining admission, he will go straight to the chancel and gaze upon those which, after all, are the only memorials of the poet which possess a really satisfying value, the monument and the tomb.

As all the world knows, the tomb is a dark slab, lying in the chancel, the inscription turned to the east. No name is given, only the lines, here copied from a photograph :—

'Good Frend for Iesvs sake forbeare
To digg the dvst encloased heare:
Blest be y^e man y^t spares thes stones,
And cvrst be he y^t moves my bones.'

AVENUE TO STRATFORD-ON-AVON CHURCH DOOR.

These lines are not the only doggerel, whether justly or unjustly, fathered upon Shakspere. The prostrate figure on a tomb in the east wall of the chancel, representing Shakspere's contemporary and intimate, John-a-Combe, suggests another stanza, even inferior in taste and diction. But we have no room now for such recollections. Above us, on the left, is the monument of the poet, coloured, according to the fashion of the time, with scarlet doublet, black, sleeveless gown, florid cheeks, and gentle hazel eyes. How Mr. Malone, the commentator, not content with 'improving' the plays, caused the bust also to be improved by a coating of white paint, how the barbarism was removed in 1861, and the statue restored, is a tale often told. The effigy certainly existed within seven years of Shakspere's death, so that, in all probability, we have a faithful representation of the poet as his contemporaries knew him. The following Latin and English inscriptions are beneath his bust :—

'Judicio Pylivm, genio socratem, arte maronem :
   terra tegit, popvlvs mæret, olympvs habet.'

   (In judgment a Nestor, in genius a Socrates, in art a Virgil : Earth covers him, the people mourns him, heaven possesses him.)

THE MONUMENT.

'STAY PASSENGER, WHY GOEST THOV BY SO
   FAST,
  READ, IF THOV CANST WHOM ENVIOVS DEATH
    HATH PLAST
  WITHIN THIS MONVMENT, SHAKSPERE, WITH
    WHOME
  QVICK NATVRE DIDE ; WHOSE NAME DOTH DECK
    Y^S TOMBE
  FAR MORE THAN COST ; SITH ALL Y^t HE HATH
    WRITT
  LEAVES LIVING ART BVT PAGE TO SERVE HIS
    WITT.

   Obiit an° Doi. 1616. Ætatis 53 die 23 Ap.'

The inscription is clumsy enough, but proves that the poet's greatness was not, as sometimes alleged, unrecognised in his own generation. The epitaph on Mistress Susanna Hall, Shakspere's favourite daughter, struck a higher note. Thus it began :—

   'Witty above her sex—but that's not all—
   Wise to salvation, was good Mistress Hall.
   Something of Shakspere was in that ; but this
   Wholly of Him with Whom she's now in bliss.'

It is to be regretted that this inscription has been effaced, to make room faith, whereof he has uttered such glorious things—admiring its beauty, but not himself entering to worship there?'

To the same effect, we may quote the preliminary sentence of Shakspere's will: 'I commend my soul into the hands of God, my Creator, hoping, and assuredly believing, through the only merits of Jesus Christ, my Saviour, to be made partaker of life everlasting.' With such a master of words, this avowal would be no mere formality. During Shakspere's last residence at Stratford, moreover, the town was under strong religious influences. Many a 'great man in Israel,' in fraternal visits to the Rev. Richard Byfield, the vicar, is said to have been hospitably entertained at New Place; and memorable evenings must have been spent in converse on the highest themes. In addition to all this, the following sonnet furnishes an interesting proof that the heart of Shakspere, at an earlier period, had not been unsusceptible to religious sentiments and aspirations:—

> 'Poor soul, the centre of my sinful earth,
>   Fooled by those rebel powers that thee array,
> Why dost thou pine within, and suffer dearth,
>   Painting thy outward walls so costly gay?
> Why so large cost, having so short a lease,
>   Dost thou upon thy fading mansion spend?
> Shall worms, inheritors of thine excess,
>   Eat up thy charge? Is this thy body's end?
> Then, soul, live thou upon thy body's loss,
>   And let·that pine to aggravate thy store;
> Buy terms divine in selling hours of dross;
>   Within be fed, without be rich no more:
> So shalt thou feed on death, that feeds on men,
>   And, death once dead, there's no more dying·then.'—*Sonnet* CXLVI.

All that such words suggest we gladly admit among the probabilities of Shakspere's unknown life. But in his dramas themselves we find no assured grasp of the highest spiritual truth, nothing to show that such truth controlled his views of life with imperial sway; little or nothing to uplift the reader from the play of human passions and the entanglement of human interests to the higher realms of Faith. It is the same Shakspere who reveals the depths of human corruption, and the nobleness of human excellence. But in portraying the latter, he stops short, and fails exactly where the higher light of faith would have enabled him to complete the delineation. His best and greatest characters are a law unto themselves: his men are passionate and strong; his women are beautiful, with a loveliness that scarcely ever reminds us of heaven: he has neither 'raised the mortal to the skies,' nor 'brought the angel down.'

We turn, then, from Stratford-on-Avon, feeling, as we have said, more deeply than ever the mystery that overhangs the career of the man, admiring, if possible, more heartily than ever the genius of the poet, and acknowledging, not without mournfulness, how much greater Shakspere might have been. For there was an inspiration within his reach that would have made him chief among the witnesses of God to men; and his magnificent endowments would then have been the richest offering ever placed by human hand upon that altar which 'sanctifieth both the giver and the gift.'

SHAKSPERE'S BIRTHPLACE BEFORE RESTORATION.

THE COUNTRY OF BUNYAN AND COWPER.

THE RIVER OUSE.

II

ON THE CANAL, AT BERKHAMPSTEAD.

'GOD gives to every man
The virtue, temper, understanding, taste,
That lifts him into life, and lets him fall
Just in the niche he was ordained to fill.

*   *   *   *   *   *

To me an unambitious mind, content
In the low vale of life.'

COWPER: *The Task*, Book iv.

THE COUNTRY OF BUNYAN AND COWPER.

YARDLEY OAK.

SOME of the most characteristic excursions through the gently undulating rural scenery which distinguishes so large a portion of the south midland district of England may be made along the towing-paths of the canals. The notion may appear unromantic; the pathway is artificial, yet it has now become rusticated and fringed with various verdure; some of the associations of the canal are anything but attractive, but upon the whole the charm is great. A wide level path, driven straight across smiling valleys and by the side of hills, here and there skirting a fair park, and occasionally bringing some broad open landscape into sudden view, with the gleam and coolness of still waters ever at the traveller's side, affords him a succession of pictures which perhaps the 'strong climber of the mountain's side' may disdain, but which to many will be all the more delightful, because they can be enjoyed with no more fatigue than that of a leisurely, health-giving stroll.

It was by such a walk as this through some of the pleasantest parts of Hertfordshire that we first made our way to Berkhampstead, the birthplace of William Cowper, turning from the canal bank to the embowered fragments of the castle, and through the quiet little town to the 'public way,'—the pretty rural by-road where the 'gardener Robin' drew his little master to school:

'Delighted with the bauble coach, and wrapped
In scarlet mantle warm, and velvet capped,'

while the fond mother watched her darling from the 'nursery window,' the memory of which one pathetic poem has made immortal.

In a well-known sentence, Lord Macaulay affirms in reference to the seven-

H 2

teenth century : 'We are not afraid to say that, though there were many clever men in England during the latter half of that century, there were only two minds which possessed the imaginative faculty in a very eminent degree. One of these minds produced the *Paradise Lost ;* the other, the *Pilgrim's Progress.'* Similarly, with regard to the brilliant literary period which began towards the close of the eighteenth century, 'we are not afraid to say' that, although there were many poets in England of no mean order, there were but two to whom it was given to view nature simply and sincerely, so as adequately to express 'the delight of man in the works of God.' One of these poets produced *The Task,* the other *The Excursion.*

When Macaulay wrote, the place of Bunyan in literature was still held

BIRTHPLACE OF COWPER, BERKHAMPSTEAD RECTORY.

a little doubtful ; the place of Cowper among poets is not wholly unquestioned now. Some are impatient of his simplicity, others scorn his piety, many cannot escape, as they read, from the shadow of the darkness in which he wrote. But we cannot doubt that, when the coming reaction from feverishness and heathenism in poetry shall have set in, the name of Cowper will win increasing honour ; men will search for themselves into the source of those bright phrases, happy allusions, 'jewels five words long, that on the stretched forefinger of all time sparkle for ever,' for which the world is often unconsciously indebted to his poems ; while his incomparable letters will remain as the finest and most brilliant specimens of an art which penny postage, telegrams, and post-cards have rendered almost extinct in England.

No one at any rate will wonder now that we should turn awhile from more outwardly striking or enchanting scenes to the ground made classic and sacred to the English Christian by the memories of Bunyan and Cowper. We may associate their names, not only from their brotherhood in faith and teaching, but from the coincidence which identifies their respective homes with one and the same river, and blends their memories with the fair still landscapes through which it steals.

The Ouse, most meandering of English streams, waters a country almost perfectly level throughout, though here and there fringed by the

OLNEY VICARAGE.

undulations of the receding Chilterns; with a picturesqueness derived from rich meadows, broad pastures with flowery hedgerows, and tall, stately trees; while in many places the still river expands into a miniature lake, with water-lilies floating upon its bosom. Among scenes like these the great dreamer passed his youth, in his village home at Elstow; often visiting the neighbouring town of Bedford, where we may picture him as leaning in many a musing fit over the old Ouse Bridge, on which the town prison then stood. The bridge is gone, the town has become a thriving modern bustling place; only the river remains, and the country walk to Elstow is little changed. There is the cottage which tradition identifies with Bunyan: with the church and the belfry, so memorable in the record of his experiences; the village green on which in his thoughtless youth he used to play at 'tip-cat:' there is nothing more to see; but it is impossible to pace through those homely ways without remembering how once the place was luminous to his awe-stricken spirit with 'the light that never was on sea or shore,' and the landscape on which his inward eye was fixed was closed in by the great white throne.

It is remarkable that there is in Bunyan's writings so little of local colouring. His fields, hills, and valleys are not of earth. The 'wilderness of this world' through which he wandered was something quite apart from the

ELSTOW GREEN.

Bedfordshire flats, although indeed 'the den' on which he lighted is but too truthful a representation of the county prison, which was so long Bunyan's 'home.'[1] Even where familiar scenes may have supplied the groundwork of the picture, incidental touches show that his soul was beyond them. His hill-sides are covered with 'vineyards;' the meadows by the river-side are fair with 'lilies;' the fruits in the orchard have mystic healing virtue. The scenery of Palestine rather than of Bedfordshire is present to his view, and his well-loved Bible has contributed as much to his descriptions as any reminiscences

[1] Dr. Brown, in his *Life of Bunyan*, has shown that the prison in which Bunyan spent twelve memorable years (1660–1672) was not the old town gaol on Ouse Bridge, but the county prison, of which only the fragment of a wall remains. But the 'Dream' *may* have come to him during a subsequent six months' confinement in the town gaol, 1675-6. The *Pilgrim's Progress* was first published 1678.

of his excursions around his native place. But it was after all in no earthly walks or haunts of men that he found the prototypes of his immortal pictures. They are idealised experiences, and from the Wicket-gate to the Land of Beulah they all represent what he had seen and felt only in his soul. No doubt the people are in many cases less abstract. A very remarkable edition of the *Pilgrim's Progress*, published some years ago by an

BEDFORD.

artist of rare promise, since deceased, portrayed the personages of the allegory in the very guise in which Bunyan must often have met their originals up and down in Bedfordshire. Such faces may be seen to-day. We ourselves thought we saw Mr. Honesty, in a brown coat, looking at some bullocks in the Bedford market-place. Ignorance tried to entice us into a theological discussion at the little country-side inn where we rested for the night: the next morning, as we passed along, Mercy was knitting at a farmhouse door, while young Mr. Brisk, driving by in his gig, made her an elaborate bow, of which we were glad to see she took the slightest possible notice.

Bedford is now at least rich in memorials of its illustrious citizen and

BUNYAN MONUMENT, BEDFORD.

prisoner for conscience sake. The Bunyan Statue, presented by the Duke of Bedford, was erected in 1874, and is one of the noblest and most characteristic out-of-door monuments in England. It has indeed been suggested that Bunyan might more appropriately have been represented in the attitude

BUNYAN GATES, BEDFORD.

WINTER-TIME.—FEEDING THE DEER IN CHATSWORTH PARK.

THE PEAK OF DERBYSHIRE.

THE traveller into Derbyshire, unaccustomed to the district, may not unnaturally inquire for 'the Peak,' which he has been taught to consider one of the chief English mountains, and the name of which has always suggested to him something like a pyramid of rock,—an English Matterhorn. He will be soon undeceived, and then may paradoxically declare the peculiarity of 'the Peak District' to be that there is *no* Peak! The range so called is a bulky mass of millstone grit, rising irregularly from the limestone formation which occupies the southern part of Derbyshire, and extending in long spurs, or arms, north and north-east into Yorkshire as far as Sheffield, and west and south into Cheshire and Staffordshire. The plateau is covered by wild moorland, clothed with fern, moss and heather, and broken up by deep hollows and glens, through which streamlets descend, each through its own belt of verdure, from the spongy morasses above, forming in their course many a minute but picturesque waterfall. The pedestrian who establishes himself in the little inn at Ashopton will have the opportunity of exploring many a breezy height and romantic glen ; while, if he has strength of limb and of lungs to make his way to Kinderscout, the highest point of all, he will breathe, at the elevation of not quite two thousand feet, as fresh and exhilarating an atmosphere as can be found anywhere in these islands; the busy smoky city of Manchester being at a distance, 'as the crow flies,' of little more than fifteen miles! It is no wonder that a select company of hard-worked men, who have lighted on this nook among the hills, having a taste for natural history, resort hither year after year, finding a refreshment in the repeated visit equal at least to that which their fellow-citizens enjoy, at greater cost, in the terraces of Buxton, or on the gigantic slope of Matlock Bank.

Where the limestone emerges from under the mass of grit, the scenery altogether changes. For roughly-rounded, dark-coloured rocks, covered with ling and bracken, now appear narrow glens, bold escarped edges, cliffs splintered into pinnacles and pierced by wonderful caves traversed by hidden streams. Of these caves the 'Peak Cavern' at Castleton is the largest, that of the 'Blue John Mine' the most beautiful, from its veins of Derbyshire spar.

The tourist, however, who confines himself to the Peak District proper, with its immediately outlying scenery, will have a very inadequate view of the charms of Derbyshire. He can scarcely do better than begin at the other extremity, ascending the Dove through its limestone valley as far as Buxton, thence taking rail to Chapel-en-le-Frith, expatiating over the Peak moorlands according to time and inclination, descending to the limestone region again at Castleton, and following the Derwent in its downward course to Ambergate, pausing in his way to visit Chatsworth and Haddon Hall, and to stay awhile at Matlock.

Having thus planned our own journey, our starting-point was Ashbourne, a quiet, pretty little town at the extremity of a branch railway. There was not much in the town itself to detain us: we could only pay a hurried visit to the church, whose beautiful spire, 212 feet high, is sometimes called the Pride of the Peak. There are some striking monuments; and among them one with an inscription of almost unequalled mournfulness. It is to an only child, a daughter: 'She was in form and intellect most exquisite. The unfortunate parents ventured their all on this frail bark, and the wreck was total.' Never was plaint of sorrowing despair more touching. Let us hope, both that the parents' darling was a lamb in the Good Shepherd's fold, and that the sorrowing father and mother found at length that there can be no total wreck to those whose treasure is in heaven!

A night's refreshing rest at the inn, where several nationalities oddly combine to make up one complex sign—the fierce Saracen, the thick-lipped negro, the English huntsman in his coat of Lincoln green!—and we sallied forth on a glorious day of early autumn to make our first acquaintance with Dovedale. Leaving the town at the extremity farthest from the railway station, we found ourselves on a well-kept, undulating road, skirted by fair pastures on either hand; the absence of cornfields being a very marked feature in the landscape. Turning into pleasant country lanes to the left, we soon reached the garden gate of a finely-situated rural inn, the

DOVEDALE.

WESTWARD HO!

CHEDDAR CLIFFS.

'PAUSE, ere we enter the long craggy vale ;
It seems the abode of solitude. So high
The rock's bleak summit frowns above our head,
Looking immediate down, we almost fear
Lest some enormous fragment should descend
With hideous sweep into the vale, and crush
The intruding visitant. No sound is here,
Save of the stream that shrills, and now and then
A cry as of faint wailing, when the kite
Comes sailing o'er the crags, or straggling lamb
Bleats for its mother.'

W. L. BOWLES.

ON THE TEIGN, DEVON.

WESTWARD HO!

ALMOST every place of popular resort has its 'season,' when its charms are supposed to be at their highest, and the annual migration of visitors sets in. The period is not always determined by climate or calendar; and such is the caprice of fashion, that many a lovely spot is left well-nigh solitary during the weeks of its full perfection, the crowd beginning to gather when the beauties of the place are on the wane. Tastes will undoubtedly differ as to the most favourable time to visit one or another beautiful scene; but none, we should imagine, will dispute our opinion that the best season for travel in the west of England is in the early spring. We leave the north, with patches of snow yet on the hills, and the first leaflets struggling in vain to unfold themselves on the blackened branches; or, if we hail from the metropolis, we gladly turn our backs on wind-swept streets and bleak suburban roads, to find ourselves in two or three hours speeding beneath soft sunshine, between far-extending orchards in all the loveliness of their delicate bloom, while the grass is of a richer tint, the blue sky, dappled with fleecy clouds, of a more exquisite purity, and instead of the slowly-relaxing grasp of winter, the promise of summer already thrills the air. 'The flowers appear on the earth; the time of the singing of birds is come, and the voice of the turtle is heard in our land.'

But whither shall we direct our steps? It is the perfection of comfort in travelling to have time at command. We need be in no haste to leave the apple-blossomy valleys of Somersetshire, even for the woods and cliffs of Devon; and if the tourist would visit a spot which, in its own way, is unique

THE GLASTONBURY THORN.

in England, let him turn aside, as we did, soon after leaving Bristol, to a rift in the Mendip Hills, and make his way through the pass between the Cheddar Cliffs. Cut sheer through the hill, from summit to base, is an extraordinary cleft. The road which winds along the bottom of the ravine is in some places only wide enough to allow two vehicles to pass abreast.